DREAMING OF...

EASTER

By Charlotte Dobson

CAN YOU FIND THE EASTER CHICK HIDDEN ON EACH PAGE?

DREAMING OF EASTER
THE SMELL WHEN MUMMY
BAKES

SHE MAKES THE TASTIEST
COOKIES
&
CAKES

CUTE LITTLE LAMBS COME OUT TO
PLAY

GAMES OF HIDE AND SEEK
WHEN MY FAMILY COMES TO

STAY

BUNNY EARS ALL
AROUND

DAFFODILS SPROUTING FROM THE

GROUND

HUNTING IN THE GARDEN FOR CHOCOLATE

EGGS

HELPING GRANDAD PLANT THE
VEG

CHURCH IS WHERE
SOME FAMILIES EASTER
IS
SPENT

FOR SOME IT MARKS THE END OF

LENT

MAYBE WE'LL DO SOME EASTER

CRAFTS

HATS...

GIFT BASKETS...

...THINGS LIKE THAT

WEARING OUR SUNDAY BEST

WINDING DOWN
FOR AN EASTER
REST

FAMILY AND FRIENDS GETTING

TOGETHER

PLAYING OUTSIDE IN NICER WEATHER

HOPPY EASTER
EVERYONE

Printed in Great Britain
by Amazon

19118099R00016